THE AMAZING ADVENTURES OF
ULYSSES

GW00992547

Mrs Russell

HOMER

**Retold by
VIVIAN WEBB and
HEATHER AMERY**

**Illustrated by
STEPHEN CARTWRIGHT**

CONTENTS

The Wooden Horse

Long ago the Greek island of Ithaca was ruled by Ulysses. His wife, Penelope, had a son called Telemachus.

One day, a beautiful Greek princess, called Helen, was captured by a foreign prince and taken to the city of Troy.

Ulysses and the other Greek kings gathered their armies. Together they sailed to Troy to rescue beautiful Helen.

The Greeks fought many battles with the Trojans, but they could not capture Troy.

They camped on the beach outside the city and tried to break down the huge walls.

After ten years, the Greek soldiers were tired of the war. "We can't win," they grumbled. "Let's go home."

But Ulysses would not give up and thought of a plan. "I know how to get into Troy," he said to the other kings.

Next day, when a Trojan sentry looked over the wall, the Greek camp was empty. "They've gone," he shouted.

The Trojans ran out on to the beach. The Greeks and their ships had gone. Nothing was left but a giant wooden horse.

"We've won, we've won! The war is over," the people shouted. "But what's this horse? It must be a gift from the Greeks."

3

The Trojans dragged the wooden horse up the hill, through the city gates and into the market square. Everyone came to stare at it.

That evening, the whole city had a party to celebrate the end of the war. There was a big feast and dancing round the horse.

When all the Trojans were in bed, a secret door in the horse opened. Ulysses and his men were hiding inside.

"Come on," Ulysses said. "But don't make a sound." They let down a rope ladder and climbed out.

They opened the city gates. Outside was the Greek army. The soldiers had sailed back to Troy during the night.

The Greek soldiers crept quietly into
the city while the Trojans were still asleep.
When they woke up, the men tried to
fight but the Greeks soon killed them all.

The Greeks made the Trojan women and
children their slaves, stole the treasure and
set fire to the city. Ulysses' plan had worked.
Helen was rescued and the war was over.

5

Cyclops, the One-Eyed Giant

After ten years of fighting, everyone wanted to go home. They shared out the treasure and sailed away. Ulysses and his men set off for their home in Ithaca.

On the way, the ship would meet many storms and pass dangerous islands. The sailors had been told that giants and monsters lived on some of these islands.

After two weeks at sea, they landed on an island to look for food and fresh water. At the top of a cliff was a big cave.

Taking a goatskin of wine, Ulysses and his men set out to explore the island. As they found no one, they climbed up the cliff.

They were tired and hungry when they reached the cave. They shouted but there was no answer. Going in, they saw huge cheeses and buckets of milk. "Let's eat and wait for the owner," said Ulysses.

Suddenly they heard a noise. A Cyclops, a one-eyed giant, was herding his sheep into the cave. Then he rolled a rock across the entrance to close it. His one eye glared at the Greeks. "Who are you?" he growled.

"We are soldiers on our way home from Troy," Ulysses said. "We came here for food and water." The giant roared and, grabbing two men, crushed them in his fists and stuffed them into his mouth.

Then the Cyclops lay down and went to sleep. The men begged Ulysses to kill the giant before he ate them all. "If we kill him; we will be trapped in here," said Ulysses. "We could not move that rock."

Next day, the giant went out of the cave but rolled back the rock again. Trapped inside, Ulysses made a plan.

He searched the cave until he found a wooden pole. After sharpening it with his sword, he hid it in a corner.

That night, when the Cyclops came home, Ulysses poured him a large bowl of wine. The giant was pleased.

"What is your name?" he asked Ulysses. "I am called Nobody," said Ulysses, and he gave the Cyclops lots more wine.

The Cyclops laughed. "Nobody is a funny name," he said. Then, after a while, drunk with all the wine, he fell asleep.

Ulysses took the pole from its hiding place and put the sharpened end in the fire to heat. Then he called quietly to his three bravest and strongest men.

Silently they crept forward, careful not to wake the Cyclops. "Now!" shouted Ulysses and they plunged the red-hot pole into the eye of the sleeping giant.

9

Everyone on the island heard the Cyclops roar with pain. They ran about, shouting "What's the matter?"

"Nobody has hurt me," the Cyclops cried. "Nobody has poked my eye out and I can't see." And he groaned loudly.

"If nobody has hurt you, why are you crying?" the giants asked. They went away saying, "He's gone mad."

The Cyclops rolled away the rock and waited outside for the Greeks to come out.

But Ulysses had thought of a way to escape. He tied the rams together in threes.

"Cling under a middle ram," he said to his men. And he drove the rams from the cave.

The Cyclops stroked the rams as they trotted past but did not feel the men underneath. Ulysses was the last to leave.

"Back to the ship," he shouted. They raced down the cliff and quickly rowed their ship away.

The giant heard the shout and knew he had been tricked again. He ran to the cliff top.

Roaring with anger, he threw rocks at the ship but missed. Ulysses and his men were safe.

Circe and her Magic Spells

Ulysses and his men sailed away, laughing at the tricks they had played on the Cyclops. They did not know that the giant was the son of Poseidon, the god of the sea.

Poseidon watched the ship, furious that the crew had hurt his son. "They are laughing now," he growled, "but they will not laugh when I take my revenge on them."

They landed safely on another island. This time Ulysses divided the crew into two groups. He and Eurylochus drew lots to see who would go in search of food and who would guard the ship.

Eurylochus won and told his men to carry their swords. He was afraid they would meet more hungry giants. They walked for hours but saw no one. The island seemed to be deserted.

Then one of the men stopped. "Look," he cried, pointing. They could see smoke rising above the trees.

"Follow me," Eurylochus said, "but be careful." They crept quietly on. At the edge of the wood was a palace.

As they stared, a beautiful woman came out and stood on the steps. "Come in," she said. "You are welcome."

She led them into a great hall where a table was already laid. "You are my guests," she said. "I have prepared a feast for you all."

The men sat round the table and began to eat. "Please tell us your name," said one of them. "I am Circe," she said, and filled their cups with wine.

Soon, full of food and wine, they began to sing and dance. They enjoyed themselves so much that no one noticed Eurylochus was not there.

Eurylochus did not trust Circe. So when the men went in the hall, he stayed outside and peeped through a window.

He saw Circe wave her magic wand and stared in horror when the men's noses turned into snouts.

Circe had changed them into grunting pigs. As she drove them out of the hall, Eurylochus turned and ran.

14

He raced back to the ship. "She has cast a spell on them," he gasped, and he told the men what he had seen. "I must rescue them," cried Ulysses and set off at once.

He had almost reached the palace when Hermes, messenger of the gods, appeared. He had been sent by the goddess Athene, who wanted Ulysses to return safely home.

Hermes said, "The lovely Athene sends you this magic flower. Eat it and you'll be safe from Circe's tricks." He gave Ulysses a white flower and flew off.

As Ulysses reached the palace, Circe came out. "Another guest, how lovely," she said. "I must be careful," thought Ulysses "but with Athene's help, I can save my men."

15

"You must be tired after your journey," Circe said. "My servants will bring food but first we will have some wine."

"I don't trust her," thought Ulysses. But he had eaten the white flower and was not afraid of Circe's magic.

"Thank you, madam," he said. While Ulysses was not looking, Circe secretly poured a potion into a cup of wine.

She waited as Ulysses drank the wine. Then she tapped his arm with her wand. Ulysses jumped up.

"Your evil magic can't harm me," he cried. Drawing his sword, he held it to her neck. "Now where are my men?"

Circe was terrified. Her magic had not worked. "I'll take you to them," she said and led him from the palace.

When they reached the pig sty, she smeared magic ointment on the pigs' snouts. Ulysses was delighted when the pigs began to change back into men.

They were frightened when they saw Circe but she promised not to turn them into pigs again. She knew Ulysses would kill her if she tried to harm his men.

In the palace a great feast was prepared and one of the men ran back to the ship to fetch the others. The feast lasted for a whole year and everyone had a good time.

When it was time for them to leave, Circe was very sad, for now she loved Ulysses. She gave him food for the journey and warned him of the dangers he would meet.

The Enchanting Sirens

The Greeks sailed away and soon came to the Sirens' island. It was surrounded by shipwrecks. The Sirens were sea nymphs who sang beautiful songs to passing sailors.

Sailors who heard their songs wrecked their ships on the rocks and drowned. No one could save them. The Sirens often lay on the rocks, waiting for a ship to sail by.

Circe had told Ulysses about the Sirens and he had a clever plan to escape from their evil spells. He cut some beeswax with his sword and gave it to his crew.

"Tie me to the mast," he told them. "I want to listen to the Sirens' song. Then plug your ears with the beeswax and row the ship past this terrible island."

When the Sirens saw the Greek ship, they gave a cry of delight and began to sing their enchanting songs.

Only Ulysses could hear them and he fell under their spell. "Untie me," he shouted as he struggled to get free.

But the ropes were tied too tightly and the crew could not hear his cries for help. Their ears were full of beeswax.

The Sirens were furious that their spell was not working. They sang louder and louder but it did not help.

They slapped their tails angrily against the rocks and sang even louder. The crew rowed steadily on.

Soon the Sirens stopped their singing. "Come back," they screamed in rage but the ship sailed safely away.

The Whirlpool

When they were far from the island, the crew untied Ulysses. As they took the wax out of their ears, they heard a great roar of water. "What's that?," they asked, afraid.

Ahead of them, a huge whirlpool swirled between two rocks. The ship had to go past it. They knew that if they went too close, it would suck them down and drown them all.

The crew ran to their places and grabbed the oars. "Row for your lives," cried Ulysses. "Steer close to the cliff."

The men pulled on the oars as hard as they could. Ulysses, feeling the tug of the water, shouted, "Pull, pull."

He looked up at the cliff. The top was hidden by cloud. He thought he saw something move and drew his sword.

In a dark cave, hidden by the cloud, lived Scylla, the six-headed monster. Hungrily she watched the ship come closer to the cliff. She stretched her necks and waited.

The men were watching the whirlpool and did not see Scylla. Suddenly, she snatched six men from the deck. "Ulysses, save us," they cried, but Scylla had swallowed them.

21

The Sea God's Revenge

The men rowed hard until they were out of Scylla's reach. Then, for the first time for four days, the wind blew and filled the sail. The tired crew were glad to rest their oars.

The wind grew stronger. Black clouds hid the sun and the lightning flashed. "Lower the sail before the mast breaks," shouted Ulysses, but it was too late.

A giant wave rolled over the ship, smashing it. Ulysses was thrown into the sea and all the men were drowned.

Ulysses clung to the broken mast. As he was lifted by a wave, he saw land. Letting go of the mast, he swam to it.

Next morning, when the sea was calm, a princess came down to the shore. She found Ulysses lying on the beach.

She took him to the king and Ulysses told him what had happened. The king promised to help him.

"Your home in Ithaca is not far," said the king. "One of my ships will take you there." The ship left that evening.

Ulysses went to sleep and did not wake up when the ship reached Ithaca. So the crew carried him to the beach.

Poseidon, the sea god, was passing in his chariot when he saw Ulysses asleep. "He should have drowned in the storm," he cried. "I will punish those who helped him."

As the ship sailed away, leaving Ulysses on the shore, Poseidon raised his hand. In a flash, the ship, the sea round it and the crew turned to rock. Poseidon smiled and rode on.

Home at Last

When Ulysses woke up on the beach, a lovely lady was standing near him. "Welcome home to Ithaca," she said. "Who are you?" asked Ulysses. "I am the lovely goddess Athene," she said.

"I have come to help you. Since you sailed to Troy twenty years ago, your wife Penelope has ruled Ithaca. Now many men think you are dead and they want to marry Penelope."

Ulysses leapt up. "I must save her," he cried. "Wait," said Athene. "These men want to kill your son, Telemachus, and are at the palace now. But I have a plan."

"Go to the palace disguised as a beggar. But first go to the swineherd's hut. I will send Telemachus there." Athene smiled and Ulysses' armour turned to beggar's rags.

Ulysses hurried down the dusty road to the swineherd's hut. "Come in, my friend, you must be hungry," the swineherd said. He thought Ulysses was a beggar.

"Have you any news?" asked the swineherd, when they had eaten. "Did you hear what happened to King Ulysses? He never came back from Troy."

Suddenly the door opened. A young man came in. "Prince Telemachus!" the swineherd gasped.

Ulysses looked at the young man. "I am your father," he said. "But you look like a beggar," said Telemachus.

"The goddess Athene disguised me," said Ulysses. "Tell me about the men who plot to steal my kingdom."

25

Next morning Ulysses went with the swineherd when he drove his pigs to the palace. "Every day the princes come to ask Queen Penelope which one of them she will marry," said the swineherd.

"She begs them to leave but they won't go away until she chooses one of them. They have been there for three years," he sighed. Ulysses hurried into the great hall where the princes were eating and drinking.

He picked up a bowl and went to the table. "I'll beg for food and find out what these princes plan to do," he thought. A fat man gave him scraps but others sent him away.

One prince threw a stool at Ulysses. Telemachus was very angry that they treated his father like a beggar. But he had promised Ulysses to wait and say nothing.

When Queen Penelope heard that a wandering beggar was in the palace, she sent her old nurse to fetch him. "This beggar may have met Ulysses on his travels," she said. "Perhaps he will have news of my husband."

Ulysses stood in the shadows. He was afraid his wife might recognize him although he was in disguise. He was heartbroken to see Penelope so sad. "Ulysses is alive and is very near to home now," he said to comfort her.

"Thank you," said Penelope. "My nurse will look after you." An old lady brought in a bowl of water.

She had known Ulysses since he was a baby. She recognized an old scar on his leg. "Ulysses," she gasped.

"Yes," he said, "but tell no one or my plan will be ruined." The nurse said, "Your secret is safe with me."

27

That night Ulysses slept on the floor of the great hall. He was woken in the morning by a maid. "Out of my way, beggar," she said. "The princes will be here soon and everything must be ready for them."

Ulysses scrambled to his feet and listened to the princes talking as they came in. "We've waited long enough," said one. "Penelope must choose one of us as her husband today. Then we will kill her son."

Just then, Penelope came in, carrying a huge ivory bow. "This bow belonged to my husband, King Ulysses," she said. "I shall marry the man who is strong enough to put the string on it."

"But first he must shoot an arrow through these twelve axes." She gave the bow to a servant and went out of the hall. Telemachus ordered a target and the axes to be set up.

The princes wanted to show how strong they were. Each one tried as hard as he could but could not string the bow.

"It's old and stiff," said one and rubbed the bow with oil. He tried again but still could not bend it enough.

At last, tired and cross, they gave up. "We'll try again tomorrow," they said. "Now bring us food and wine."

Ulysses stepped forward. "May I try?" he asked. The princes laughed. "A beggar wants to be king," one said.

Ulysses picked up the bow and, bending it easily, put on the string. He took an arrow, pulled the string and fired.

The arrow shot through the axes and right into the centre of the target. The princes watched in horror.

29

The goddess Athene had changed into a sparrow and was watching from the ceiling. As soon as the arrow hit the target, she turned Ulysses' rags back into armour.

"I am Ulysses," he cried, taking another arrow. "I have come back for my revenge." And he shot a prince dead.

Telemachus drew his sword and ran to help his father. The princes tried to escape but a servant had locked the doors.

The princes fought hard but Ulysses and Telemachus killed them all. Then the old nurse, who had hidden behind a pillar, ran to tell Penelope what had happened.

Penelope hurried into the hall. "How do I know you are Ulysses?" she asked. "Perhaps the gods are playing a trick on me. Perhaps they have made a beggar look just like my husband."

Then she thought of a test. "Go and move the big bed into the other room," she said to the nurse. "Wait," cried Ulysses, "the bed can't be moved. I built it round a tree."

"That proves you are Ulysses," said Penelope, smiling. "Only you know about the tree." "Yes, my dear, faithful wife," said Ulysses, "I have come home safely at last. And I shall tell you and my brave son, Telemachus, of all my strange and amazing adventures."

About the story of Ulysses

The story of Ulysses is a very old one. It was written, probably about 3,000 years ago, by Homer, a Greek poet and storyteller. The Greeks loved to listen to stories about gods and heroes.

In Homer's story, called *The Odyssey*, Ulysses is known as Odysseus. In this book, he is given his Roman and more common name of Ulysses.

Troy, the city of the Trojans, on the coast of what is now Turkey, was about 1,000 kilometres by sea from Ithaca.

The Greeks believed in many gods and goddesses, who lived on Mount Olympus. These gods sometimes helped people but sometimes they played nasty tricks on them. They were very powerful and could turn themselves into animals, birds or trees.

Athene was the daughter of the chief god, Zeus. Like other gods, she was not always clever or very wise.

Poseidon was the god of the sea and earthquakes. The Romans called him Neptune.

Further Reading

If you have enjoyed reading about Ulysses, here are some other books of Greek stories.

The Odyssey of Homer by Barbara L. Picard (Oxford University Press)

The Iliad of Homer Barbara L. Picard (Oxford University Press)

Giants and Warriors by James Reeves (Blackie & Sons Ltd)

The God Beneath the Sea by Leon Garfield and Edward Blishen (Longmans)

THE AMAZING ADVENTURES OF
HERCULES

Retold by
CLAUDIA ZEFF

Illustrated by
STEPHEN CARTWRIGHT

CONTENTS

Series Editor: Heather Amery

Reading Expert: Betty Root
Centre for the Teaching of Reading
University of Reading

An Evil Spell

Long ago in Greece, the great god Zeus had a baby son called Hercules. All the gods and goddesses came to see the baby and decided that they would make him very strong and brave. But the goddess Hera was jealous of Hercules and wanted to harm him.

One day, she made two deadly snakes crawl into Hercules' cradle. He was already so strong he strangled them both.

By the time he was fifteen, Hercules could shoot arrows further and wrestle better than any man or god.

When he left school, he worked on a farm. But he was soon bored and longed to go off on an adventure.

Then, one day, he met a messenger who told him that a wicked lord was stealing the King of Thebes' cows.

Hercules went to Thebes and challenged the lord to a battle. The whole army marched out to fight him.

But Hercules had a plan. He waited on a narrow path. As the soldiers came along, one by one, he killed them.

The King of Thebes was so pleased, he said, "You may marry Megera, my daughter, and live in my palace."

Hercules lived happily with Megera and they had three fine sons. He taught them to shoot, to wrestle and to drive racing chariots.

But the goddess Hera was watching him angrily. "I'll put an evil spell on him," she thought, "and make him do something terrible."

Suddenly, Hercules went mad and killed his sons. When the spell was over, he was heartbroken and went to the temple to beg forgiveness.

The First Task

"The gods will forgive you," the temple priestess said, "if you do twelve tasks for King Eurystheus of Tiryns."

So Hercules went to Tiryns. The King said, "There is a huge lion about. Your first task is to kill it."

Hercules set off to look for the lion. He searched for a whole month before he found its giant footprints.

Following the tracks, he saw a lion prowling about near a cave. He hid and waited until it came close.

Then, drawing his sword, he jumped out and struck it. But the lion's skin was so thick, the sword only bent.

The lion roared, ready to bite, when Hercules gave it such a mighty blow with his club it sat down, stunned.

Then it slunk into a cave. Hercules crept after it. Suddenly, the lion sprang on him out of the darkness.

Hercules fell down with the lion on top of him. He fought it for hours until, at last, he strangled it.

Then he dragged the dead beast out of the cave. Using all his strength, he lifted it on to his huge shoulders.

He carried the lion back to the King and laid it at his feet. "Take the nasty thing away," screamed the King.

He was so frightened, he jumped into a big brass pot. And he would not come out until the lion had gone.

Hercules made the lion's skin into a cloak. It was so thick and tough, it saved his life many times.

The Nine-Headed Monster

"Your next task," the King said, "is to go to the Argos marsh and kill the Hydra, a deadly nine-headed monster."

Hercules asked Iolaus, his nephew, to go with him. Next day, they drove across the dark, stinking marsh.

Suddenly, the goddess Athene appeared and pointed to the Hydra's cave. "Only flaming arrows will make it come out of its lair," she said.

"And when you go near it, hold your breath or one sniff of its poison will kill you." Before Hercules could thank her, she disappeared.

"Come on," he said to Iolaus, "but be careful." He tied bunches of grass to his arrows, set fire to them and shot them into the cave.

Swinging his club, he hit one head with all his might. The head screamed and fell off with a terrible thud.

But as it fell, two new heads sprouted up in its place. Hercules stared for a moment, then ran back to Iolaus.

The monster crawled out hissing angrily, its nine heads spitting poison. Hercules held his breath and raced towards it.

"Quick," he shouted, "set fire to my spear." Then he hacked off the heads, one by one, burning the necks so new heads could not grow.

At last the Hydra was dead. Hercules dipped his arrows in its blood. "It is deadly poison," he said, "but it may be useful to me some day."

The Stag with Golden Antlers

Hercules went to the King for his third task. "Now find the Stag with Golden Antlers and bring it to me unharmed," said the King.

"The swiftest and most beautiful of all deer, it is protected by the goddess Artemis. She has sworn to kill anyone who hurts it."

Hercules set off at once and chased the stag for a whole year. He was not allowed to shoot it and it ran so fast he could not catch it.

Then one day, when he was by a river, he saw something shining in the bushes. It was the golden antlers.

Picking up his net, he crept silently down the river bank. The stag did not see him and stood still, drinking.

Hercules leapt towards it and threw his net over it. The stag tried to escape but it was trapped.

It fought and struggled until it was tired out. When it lay still, Hercules gently tied up its golden hooves.

Then he lifted the stag on to his back and started on the long journey to Tiryns. Suddenly he saw a woman standing in his way.

"Stop," she cried. "I am the goddess Artemis. Where are you taking my stag?" To King Eurystheus," said Hercules. "I will not hurt it."

"Show the stag to the King," said Artemis. "Then you must bring it back." Hercules promised to obey her and set off again for Tiryns.

The Giant Wild Boar

Hercules carried the stag to the King and then set it free in the forest. For his next task he had to capture a huge wild boar alive.

On his way to find it, he met some centaurs, strange creatures who were half men and half horses. "You are welcome," they said.

They took him into a great cave and prepared a feast in his honour. Soon they were so busy eating and drinking

they did not notice other centaurs creeping up. These wild centaurs had come to steal the food and wine.

Suddenly they attacked, hurling rocks into the cave. Grabbing his bow, Hercules fired his poison arrows at them, killing them all.

The boar was so big, it was clumsy and slow. Keeping at a safe distance, Hercules drove it in front of him.

Slowly he drove it up and up until they reached the snow. When the boar fell into a snowdrift, it was trapped.

Next morning, Hercules set off again in search of the boar. At last he found it high up on a mountain. He thought of a clever plan.

Hercules leapt on it and quickly tied it up with chains. Then, staggering under its tremendous weight, he carried it to Tiryns.

When the King saw the boar's huge tusks, he jumped into his brass pot again. He was so frightened, he would not come out for three days.

Cleaning the Stables

When at last the King came out of his pot, he said to Hercules, "Don't bring any more nasty animals in here."

"Your next task is to go to King Augeas and clean out his stables in one day. This time you won't succeed."

King Augeas laughed when he heard what Hercules had to do. "Your task is impossible," he said.

"Come and look at my stables. They have not been cleaned out for thirty years." Hercules stared at all the smelly mess and thought hard.

Next day at dawn, when the cows were out in the fields, he started work. First he knocked a big hole in each end of the long stables.

Then he climbed up the hill behind the stables. There two rivers met and flowed down a valley. He looked at them and smiled to himself.

44

All day he worked in the hot sun, carrying huge rocks to dam the rivers and change their courses.

When he had finished, the rivers flowed together and poured straight down the hill towards the stables.

Hercules watched as the water gushed through the holes in the walls. It washed out all the mess and carried it away to the sea.

Just before sunset, he changed the course of the rivers again and mended the walls. The stables were bright and clean.

Deadly Birds

Hercules sixth task was to kill a flock of terrible birds. They had wings, beaks and claws of brass and they ate people and animals.

After trudging through a thick forest, Hercules came to a deep marsh. The birds lived on an island in the middle of a marsh.

Hercules found a boat and tried to row it to the island. But the oars stuck in the thick mud and the boat would not move.

He sat down and wondered what to do. He could not wade to the island and the birds were too far away to shoot from the bank.

So he prayed to the goddess Athene for help. In a flash she appeared in front of him, holding a golden rattle. "Take this," she said.

"It is magic. Shake it and its terrible noise will frighten the birds. When they fly away, shoot them with your poisonous arrows."

Hercules took the rattle but before he could thank Athene for her help, she vanished in another flash.

Holding the rattle above his head, Hercules shook it as hard as he could. He was almost deafened by the terrible noise.

On the island, the birds rose into the air, screaming and shrieking. As they flew over his head, he shot them down, one by one.

When they were all dead, he picked up the two biggest birds. Careful of their sharp beaks, he took them to show to King Eurystheus.

The Great Bull of Crete

The King looked at them and said, "They don't seem very dangerous. Now you must fetch a really fierce beast."

"It is the great white bull of Crete which belongs to King Minos." Hercules went to the harbour to find a ship.

With his crew, he sailed south until he came to the steep cliffs of Crete and landed on the island.

He climbed up the cliff and at the top he stopped to stare at the magnificent palace of King Minos.

King Minos welcomed him and took him into a hall. There they feasted together. "I have come for your great white bull," said Hercules.

"Please take it," said the King. "It is killing my people and destroying my island. But be warned. It is not an ordinary bull."

Hercules went in search of the bull and found it in an olive grove. He had never seen anything so fierce.

He crept up to it. The bull turned towards him, pawing the ground and breathing flames from its huge nostrils.

But Hercules was protected by his lion's skin. As the bull charged, he grabbed its horns and clung on while it tried to toss and gore him.

At last, it was so tired out Hercules could drag it to his ship. When King Eurystheus saw the bull he jumped into his pot again.

Man-Eating Horses

When the King came out, he said to Hercules, "Your next task is to bring me the horses of King Diomedes. He feeds them with people."

Hercules set off with four friends for Diomedes' castle. The King welcomed them but Hercules did not trust him. He warned his friends.

"The King plans to kill us when we are asleep," he said. That night, they climbed out of a bedroom window and went to the stables.

Silently, the men crept to where the guards stood dozing outside the stables and knocked them out.

Then they broke down the stable doors and rushed in. The savage horses were chained to a wooden beam.

While the horses snorted and stamped, Hercules quickly chopped down the beam to free their iron chains.

"Come on," he cried and he and his men drove the horses down to the ship. As they reached the beach, they heard Diomedes shouting angrily.

"You take charge of the horses," Hercules shouted to one of his friends. "The rest of you get ready to fight the King's soldiers."

Diomedes and his guards charged towards them armed with swords and shields. Hercules and his men fought them on the seashore.

They quickly defeated the guards. Hercules killed Diomedes and dragged his body along the beach.

When he reached the horses, he found they had eaten his friend. He was so angry, he fed Diomedes to them.

After they had eaten the King, they grew quite tame. Hercules led them to his ship and sailed back to Tiryns.

The Amazon's Belt

The King was terrified of the horses. "Take them away," he screamed. When they had gone, he said, "Now I will give you your ninth task."

"My daughter wants you to bring her the belt Hippolyta always wears. She is the Queen of the Amazons who are fierce women fighters."

All the young men in Tiryns begged Hercules to take them with him. They had heard stories of the Amazons but no one had ever seen them.

Choosing the bravest men, Hercules set off in his ship. They were all excited but a little afraid of meeting the women fighters.

After many days at sea, they saw land. As they came near the shore, the men put on their armour and swords.

But, to their surprise, Hippolyta came down to the beach to meet them. "You are welcome," she said.

52

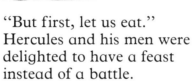

Hercules told her why they had come. "Put away your swords," she said. "I'll give you my belt as a present."

"But first, let us eat." Hercules and his men were delighted to have a feast instead of a battle.

The goddess Hera watched them secretly. She was angry that Hercules was safe and enjoying himself.

Disguising herself as an Amazon, she whispered to the women, "Hercules has come to kill our Queen."

The women grabbed their swords and attacked Hercules and his men. "We have been tricked," shouted Hercules.

"Back to the ship." In the fight, he killed Hippolyta, stole her belt and then ran after his men to the beach.

The Amazon women jumped on their huge war horses and charged after them.

Hercules' men were afraid of these fierce women but they fought hard and bravely.

The battle went on all the afternoon and many of the men were badly wounded.

Hercules lifted his wounded men on to the ship and then set sail back to Tiryns.

On the way, the men tended their wounds and Hercules kept the precious belt safe.

The Amazons were winning until Hercules shot them all with his poisonous arrows.

When they reached Tiryns, Hercules went at once to King Eurystheus. His daughter was delighted with the belt.

She wanted to reward Hercules but the King said, "Don't be silly. He has still three more tasks to do."

The Ogre's Cows

"Now you must find Geryon, the three-headed ogre, and bring me his cows," the King said to Hercules. "He lives on an island near Africa."

Hercules walked all the way from Greece to Gibraltar. There he crossed the sea and walked along the African coast in the burning sun.

One afternoon, he was so hot and cross, he shot an arrow at the sun. Helios, the sun god, felt sorry for him and cooled the sun's rays.

When, at last, Hercules saw the island, Helios sent down his sun chariot which was like a giant water lily.

Hercules climbed in and, holding up his lion's skin for a sail, drifted across the sea to Geryon's island.

He left his strange boat on the beach and set out to explore. Soon he saw the cows on a hill and climbed up.

He went on to where the cows were grazing. There, standing in the field, was the great three-headed ogre, Geryon.

Hercules hid behind a rock and stared at the monster. Then he quietly fitted a poisonous arrow to his bow.

When he reached the top, a snarling two-headed dog leapt out at him. Hercules swung his club and, with a mighty blow, killed it.

"Geryon," he shouted, coming out of his hiding place. The ogre turned and Hercules shot him dead, with the arrow through all three bodies.

Hercules drove the cows on to the sun chariot and sailed back to Tiryns. But King Eurystheus only grumbled that he had taken so long.

The Golden Apples

Hercules still had two more tasks to do. The next one was to find the Tree of the Hesperides and pick three of its golden apples.

He begged the goddess Athene to tell him where the Tree was. "Go to the end of the Earth," she said. "There you will find the magic Tree."

After walking for months and months, he came at last to the Earth's end. There the giant Atlas held up the sky with his mighty arms.

Hercules asked him what he should do. "You must kill the dragon which guards the Tree," said Atlas. "But only I can pick the apples."

When he reached the Tree, Hercules saw a golden dragon with golden eyes glaring at him. He shot it dead through its neck.

58

"Now hold up the sky for me while I go to the Tree," said Atlas. He moved the great load on to Hercules and hurried down the valley.

Hercules groaned under the weight of the sky. It seemed like hours before Atlas came back with the three golden apples.

"If you hold up the sky for a little longer, I will go to the King," Atlas said. Hercules knew it was a trick. Atlas would never come back.

"Thank you," said Hercules, "but first show me how to hold it." "Like this," said Atlas, taking it. Hercules walked off with the apples.

Dog of the Underworld

Hercules went slowly back to Tiryns. He had been working on his tasks for ten years and longed to finish them. He gave the golden apples to the King who said, "Your last task is the hardest. You must capture Cerberus, the three-headed dog which guards the Underworld."

Hercules did not know the way to the Underworld. But the gods sent Hermes, their winged messenger, and Athene to guide him there.

They led him down many long dark tunnels until they came to the black River Styx. They had to cross it to reach the Underworld.

The old boatman, Charon, was waiting to ferry people across. "I can only take the ghosts of dead people in my boat," he said crossly.

Hermes argued with him until he said, "All right. I will take Hercules but I won't take you or Athene." Hercules got into the boat.

On the other side of the Styx was the grey land of the dead. Hercules stepped out of the boat and walked past all the ghosts. They drifted round him, staring at the only living man in the dead Underworld.

Suddenly, he saw the snaky head of Medusa who used to turn people to stone. Now she was a harmless ghost.

He walked on through the silent grey mist. At last he saw the King and Queen of the Underworld, sitting on their grey thrones.

Kneeling down, he begged, "Please may I take Cerberus away?" "You may take the dog as long as you do not hurt it," said the King.

Hercules hurried back to the dark River Styx. There stood the terrible three-headed dog, guarding the gates of the Underworld.

Cerberus struggled to get free but Hercules held on to its three heads. Its tail lashed and bit him but he only tightened his grip.

Cerberus raised its three heads, each one with a mane of hissing snakes, and lashed its snaky tail. Hercules stepped nearer.

The dog snarled and leapt in the air. Hercules crouched, waiting. Then he suddenly rushed forward and flung himself on the dog.

After hours of fighting, the dog sank to the ground, exhausted. Hercules dragged it to the River Styx and crossed over in the boat.

Hermes and Athene were waiting there and helped him take Cerberus to Tiryns. He carried the dog into the palace and threw it down.

"Here is Cerberus. I have finished my twelve tasks," he said to the King. Snarling and hissing, the dog ran forward.

With a scream of terror, Eurystheus jumped into his brass pot. Hercules grabbed Cerberus and carried him back to the Underworld.

Then he went to the temple and knelt in front of the priestess. "Hercules," she said. "You are now forgiven for killing your three sons."

The gods were so pleased with Hercules they welcomed him to Mount Olympus. "You have proved you are strong and very brave," they said.

"You may stand next to your father, Zeus." And when he went on more adventures, the gods watched over Hercules and made sure he was safe.

About the story of Hercules

The story of Hercules was first told about 3,000 years ago in Greece. The Greeks had many heroes but Hercules was the strongest. They called him Heracles. Hercules was his Roman name.

Hera was the wife of Zeus. She was often jealous and bad-tempered, but she was very powerful.

The city of Tiryns, where Eurystheus lived, was on the east coast of Greece.

Zeus, the chief god, ruled the sky and often carried a thunderbolt with him. He lived on Mount Olympus with the other gods and goddesses.

Atlas was punished by Zeus for making war on the gods. In some stories Atlas holds up the whole world. An atlas, a book which holds maps of the world, is named after him.

The King of the Underworld was called Hades. He kidnapped the lovely Persephone to be his Queen.

Further Reading

If you have enjoyed reading about Hercules, here are some other books of Greek stories.

Gods, Men and Monsters from Greek Myths
by Michael Gibson
(Peter Lowe)

Tales of the Greek Heroes
by Roger Lancelyn Green
(Puffin)

Heroes and Monsters
by James Reeves
(Blackie & Sons Ltd)

Favourite Greek Myths
by Lilian S. Hyde
(Harrap)

THE AMAZING ADVENTURES OF
JASON
& THE GOLDEN FLEECE

**Retold by
CLAUDIA ZEFF**

**Illustrated by
STEPHEN CARTWRIGHT**

CONTENTS

Series Editor: Heather Amery

Reading Expert: Betty Root
Centre for the Teaching of Reading
University of Reading

King Pelias' Throne

Long ago in Greece, there was a boy called Jason. His father had been King of Iolcos until his Uncle Pelias stole the throne.

Jason's father sent him away to school. His teacher was a wise old centaur, half man and half horse. He was called Chiron.

One day Chiron said, "Jason, you are now old enough to go back to Iolcos. You must win back your throne from your Uncle Pelias."

Jason set off at once. On his way he came to a river. Sitting on the bank was an old woman. "Please help me across the water," she cried.

"I will," said Jason, and he put her on his back and waded across the river. When he reached the other side, he found he had lost a sandal.

He wanted to look for it but the woman said, "Don't stop. Continue your journey with one sandal and you will become a great hero."

Jason turned to ask her what she meant, but the woman had disappeared. So he went on his way and soon he came to the gates of Iolcos.

Everyone stared at him as he walked through the city. They all wondered who the stranger was. Jason went to King Pelias' palace.

Pelias was horrified to see Jason. He had been warned by the gods that a young man, wearing one sandal, would come to take his throne.

"I know why you are here," the King said to Jason. "You may have my throne if you can bring me the precious Golden Fleece."

The Fleece was far away in Colchis. The journey would be very dangerous but Jason agreed to go. A shipbuilder called Argus built him a

beautiful ship. When it was finished, the goddess Athene appeared. "Take this magic branch," she said to Jason. "It will protect your ship."

The Voyage Begins

The ship was called the Argo and the magic branch was fixed to its bow. Everyone for miles around heard about Jason's voyage

They all wanted to go with him to find the Golden Fleece. Princes, heroes and the sons of gods all gathered at the harbour.

Jason had to choose who he would take with him. First came Orpheus. He played the lyre and sang so sweetly, the animals came to listen.

Then came Atlanta, the beautiful huntress. She was followed by Hercules, the strongest man in the world.

Next were the twin sons of the North Wind. They had gold wings on their ankles and could fly like birds.

Jason agreed to take them all and many more. There were fifty altogether. Jason called them the Argonauts.

Everything was now ready for the long voyage. All the people of Iolcos came to see the ship set sail.

Orpheus stood on the bow and played his lyre. Even the fish came up to listen to his enchanting music.

At first the sea was so rough, the crew struggled to row the ship. Then the gods came to their aid and sent a great gust of wind. It filled the sail and drove the ship out of the harbour into the open sea.

Amycus the Bully

The Argo sailed north for three days. Then the crew stopped at an island for food and fresh water.

A huge man stood on the beach, his great muscular body covered with hair. He strode towards the ship.

"I am King Amycus," he said. "Anyone who comes to my island has to fight me. No one has beaten me yet."

One of the Argonauts came forward. "I am Polydeuces. I will fight you to the death," he said bravely.

The great bully looked at Polydeuces and laughed. "You can't fight me," he roared. "You're only half my size."

Jason tried to stop Polydeuces but he took off his cloak. "Hold this for me, Jason," he said calmly.

The Argonauts and the King's men gathered round to watch the fight. Amycus raised his huge fists and tried to hit Polydeuces. But Polydeuces

darted out of his way. For hours Polydeuces dodged the blows, until the King was tired out and the sun was low in the sky.

Polydeuces cleverly moved round until the sun shone straight into the King's eyes. Amycus was blinded and he stumbled.

As he fell, Polydeuces gave him a great blow on the head. Amycus groaned and dropped to the ground, dead.

The King's men grabbed their spears and clubs. Shouting angrily, they charged towards Polydeuces.

"Quick, run," shouted Jason. All the Argonauts rushed back to the ship and safely escaped from the island.

The Wise Old Man

The Argonauts sailed north towards the Black Sea. One day, the wind blew in great gusts and the sky grew dark. As they lowered the sail, the thunder crashed. Huge waves tossed the ship and swept it on to a rocky island. Then, after many hours, the storm was over.

Jason climbed on to the shore. All the crew were safe and the ship was not damaged. Jason and two men went to explore the island.

After a while, they came to a very old house. Slowly they pushed open the door and peered inside. It looked very dark and gloomy.

Then they heard a tapping noise. A blind old man with a stick hobbled down the steps. "Who are you? What do you want?" he cried.

Jason knew this was the wise old man, Phineas, who could see into the future. "I am Jason," he said. "Tell me what dangers we will meet."

"I will if you get rid of the Harpies," said Phineas. "They eat all my food." Jason agreed and sent for the sons of the North Wind.

Phineas laid a feast as a trap. The Harpies swooped down at once. They were birds like vultures, with women's heads. The winged twins flew into the air and attacked the Harpies with their swords. Screaming, the Harpies tried to escape but the twins killed them.

Clashing Rocks

"The birds are dead and you can eat in peace," said Jason. "Thank you," said Phineas. "Now listen to what I have to tell you."

"Beware of the Clashing Rocks in the Black Sea. If they clash together when the Argo sails between them, you will be crushed."

Phineas gave Jason a white dove. "When you reach the Rocks, let it go. If it flies through safely, you will also be safe."

Jason and his men thanked the wise old man and went back to the shore. They boarded the Argo and rowed away from Phineas' island.

The next day, they reached the great Clashing Rocks at the entrance to the Black Sea. Jason held up the dove and let it go.

74

Jason gave the order to start rowing. But the wind was against the Argo and the great Rocks began to move slowly together.

The goddess Athene saw that the ship was in danger. She sent a huge wave to push it through the gap. "Row for your lives," shouted Jason.

The bird flew straight for the Rocks. As it fluttered between them, they clashed together. But they caught only one tail feather.

As the ship raced through, the Rocks clashed together. But they only caught one plank of the stern.

Then Athene used her magic to calm the sea. That evening the Argo sailed safely into the Black Sea.

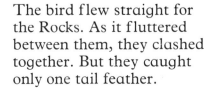

Colchis at Last

Next day a flock of huge, ugly birds flew over the ship. Suddenly one of the crew cried out. A dart was sticking in his shoulder.

Phineas had warned Jason of these dangerous birds which attacked and ate people. They could shoot poisonous darts from their wings.

Jason knew that his arrows would not kill the birds. He ordered half the crew to row and the rest to hold shields above their heads.

"Make as much noise as you can to scare the birds," said Jason. They all shouted as loudly as they could and the birds flew quickly away.

The Argo's Voyage

That night, the Argo reached the broad river which led to Colchis. It sailed past the great Caucasian Mountains towards the city.

Jason and his Argonauts were delighted that the long voyage from Iolcos was over.

MOUNT OLYMPUS

IOLCOS

GREECE

SPARTA

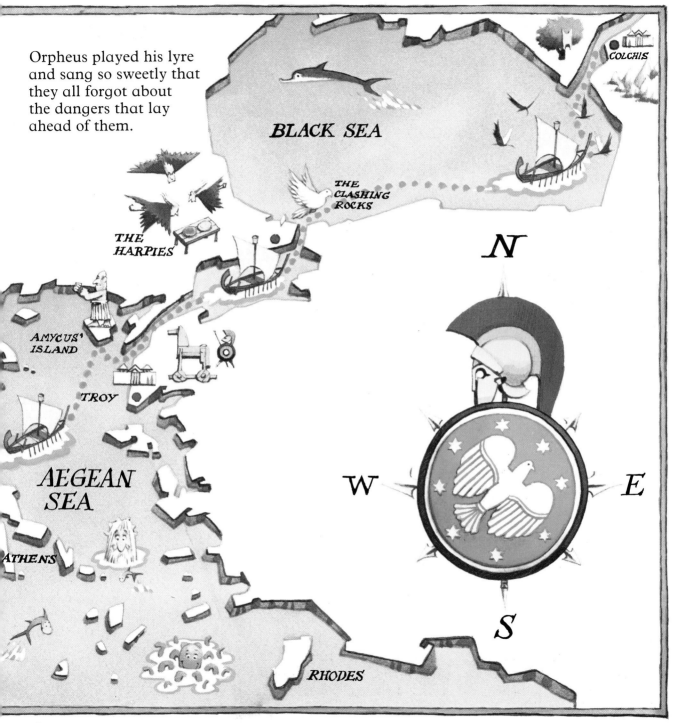

Orpheus played his lyre and sang so sweetly that they all forgot about the dangers that lay ahead of them.

COLCHIS

BLACK SEA

THE CLASHING ROCKS

THE HARPIES

N

AMYCUS' ISLAND

TROY

AEGEAN SEA

W

E

ATHENS

S

RHODES

Princess Medea

Jason ordered his crew to anchor the Argo just out of sight of Colchis.

The Argonauts rowed the ship into some reeds. There they waited until daylight.

In the morning, Jason went with two men to see Aeetes, the King of Colchis.

They arrived at his palace and went into a beautiful courtyard. King Aeetes walked out to greet them.

"I have come to fetch the Golden Fleece and take it to King Pelias. Then I can claim my throne," said Jason.

"You may have the Fleece if you do the tasks I set for you," said the King, with a cunning smile.

"First you must tame two bulls and then plough a field with them," he said. "Next you must sow the field with dragon's teeth."

"I will do the tasks," said Jason, bravely. But his men looked very worried. They were afraid the bulls would trample Jason to death.

The King's family came out of the palace to meet the strangers. The King's daughter, Medea, was there. She had magic powers.

As soon as she saw Jason, she fell in love with him. "I must do something to help this brave young man," she said to herself.

Jason went back to the ship feeling very sad. He told the crew what he had to do.

They all wanted to help him but no one could think of any clever plan.

In the palace, Medea cried. She wanted to help Jason but was scared of the King.

Then she had an idea. She waited until everyone was asleep and crept out of the palace to the stables.

"I will go to the temple and pray to Hecate, the goddess of witchcraft and magic," Medea thought.

Silently, she harnessed a mule to her chariot. Then she drove through the woods to Hecate's temple.

In the temple Medea lit the lamps and knelt in front of the altar. She prayed to the goddess for help.

Hecate told her to pick some herbs in the wood and make a magic potion. Medea did as Hecate said.

She found the herbs and made a paste, chanting a magic spell. Then she went to look for Jason.

He was walking alone in the wood. He had to fight the bulls at dawn and had less then two hours to think of a way to beat them.

Medea ran up to Jason. "Drink this magic potion before you fight the bulls," she whispered. "Its magic powers will protect you."

"Thank you for your help, princess," said Jason. "I will do as you say." He kissed Medea's hand and went on his way.

The Fire-Breathing Bulls

At sunrise, the Argonauts and the people of Colchis crowded round the field which Jason had to plough.

King Aeetes and Medea came to watch. Jason drank the magic potion and bravely walked into the field.

He peered into the bulls' cave. They bellowed and stamped, shaking the ground beneath Jason's feet.

Suddenly the bulls charged out, pounding the earth with their huge brass hooves and breathing flames.

The scorching flames shot all round Jason. They burnt the earth near his feet but they did not harm him.

Medea's magic potion was working. Jason grew braver and walked right up to the terrifying bulls.

He grabbed them by their horns and forced them down until they were kneeling. Then he stroked them.

The bulls became calm and snorted happily. The people watched in silence. They could not believe their eyes.

Jason slipped the yoke over the bulls' necks and led them to the plough. Soon he had ploughed the field.

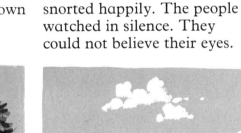

King Aeetes was furious that Jason had tamed the bulls so easily. He gave Jason a helmet full of dragon's teeth.

Jason took the helmet and walked up and down the field, sowing the teeth. All day he worked in the hot sun.

It was late when he had finished and the sun was setting. Jason felt very tired and thirsty.

The Dragon's Teeth

He walked to a river near the field for a drink of water. Suddenly he heard the crowd shouting.

He turned round. Soldiers with swords and spears were springing up where he had sowed the dragon's teeth.

Jason quickly thought of a plan. He waited until the field was full of soldiers and they were ready to fight.

Then he picked up a huge boulder from the river bank. Using all his strength, he threw it into the field.

The boulder landed in the middle of the soldiers, killing one of them. Jason hid and watched.

The soldiers looked round to see who had attacked them. But they could not see anyone. They started arguing about who had thrown the boulder, waving their swords and spears. Then they began to fight. Jason watched the fierce battle from his hiding place. Soon most of the soldiers were wounded or dead.

85

Jason rushed on to the field and quickly killed the rest of the soldiers.

The Argonauts crowded round him, cheering. All the people of Colchis cheered too.

Medea did not dare to look pleased. She was afraid her father would suspect her.

The King went up to Jason. "Now we will see if you can fight the serpent that guards the Golden Fleece," he said.

Aeetes was sure no one could kill the terrible serpent that lay coiled around the tree of the Golden Fleece.

He climbed into his chariot, smiling to himself. Then he drove off to the city in a great cloud of dust.

At the palace the King paced up and down. He was afraid Jason had magic powers and would take the Fleece.

Suddenly he had an idea and called his messenger. "Bring my army to the palace at once," he ordered.

When the army was lined up in front of him, he said, "Tonight I want you to burn the Argo and all her crew."

Medea was hiding behind a pillar and overheard him. Horrified, she ran from the palace as fast as she could.

The Golden Fleece

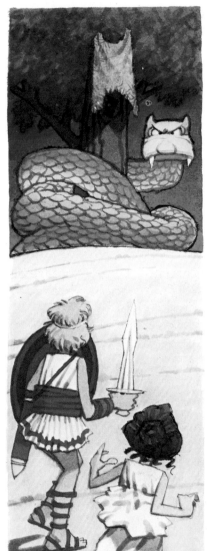

Medea ran all the way to the Argo. "Jason, Jason," she called. "We must go at once to find the Fleece."

"My father is plotting to burn your ship tonight." Jason leapt up and put on his sword and shield.

He called the Argonauts. "Row the ship away and hide it where the King's men can't find you," he said.

Then he and Medea set off into the dark woods. At last they came to a clearing. There stood a huge oak tree.

Hanging from one of its branches was the shining Golden Fleece. The serpent lay coiled round the trunk.

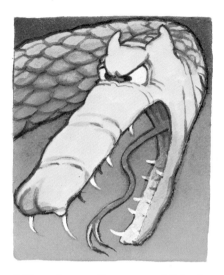

When it saw Jason and Medea the great serpent slithered towards them. It hissed, showing its fangs, and its scales rattled as it moved.

Medea bravely stood in front of the serpent and began to sing. She sang the words of a magic spell which would send the serpent to sleep.

Enchanted by the spell, the serpent slowly closed its eyes and fell asleep. "Quick, before it wakes up," Medea whispered to Jason.

Jason climbed up the serpent's coils to the top of the tree. He grabbed the Golden Fleece and carefully unhooked it from the branch.

A Narrow Escape

Jason and Medea rushed back through the woods to the Argo. Jason held up the Fleece, its golden wool glistening in the moonlight.

The Argonauts stared at it in wonder. "We must go as quickly as we can," Jason said. "If we stay here, we are in great danger."

They set sail for Iolcos, taking Medea with them. But the King's guards saw the Argo leave and ran to the palace to tell the King.

Aeetes was furious. "Jason must not escape," he shouted. "I will kill him and take back the Golden Fleece."

He ordered his fastest ships to be made ready and called all the men of Colchis to the palace.

"We must find the Argo and fight for the Fleece," he cried. The men cheered and followed him to the shore.

The men of Colchis put on their armour, then boarded the ships and set off to find Jason and his crew.

They chased the Argo to the Black Sea. Their ships were smaller and could sail faster than Jason's.

By noon, the little ships had almost caught up with the Argo. Jason saw them in the distance. "Row!" he shouted.

But the wind was against the Argonauts and Aeetes' ships came nearer and nearer. Soon they surrounded the Argo.

The Argonauts were trapped. "We cannot fight them all," cried Jason. "We will have to give up the Fleece." But then Medea whispered to him.

"My brother, Asbyrtus, is commander of the ships," she said. "If we kill him, my father will give up. It is our only chance."

Jason agreed and shouted to Aeetes' ships, "Asbyrtus, come aboard and we'll make a truce." Asbyrtus climbed on to the Argo.

While he was talking to Jason, Medea took out a small dagger. She crept up behind her brother and stabbed him in the back.

One of the Colchian men heard Asbyrtus cry out. "King Aeetes," the man called, "your son is in great danger."

The King stood on his ship and, weeping for his dead son, he cursed his daughter.

Jason was ashamed of what he and Medea had done. But they still had to escape.

King Aeetes rushed to the deck as Medea pushed Asbyrtus' body over the side of the Argo and into the sea.

Aeetes ordered his crew to rescue the body of his son. In the confusion, the Argo slipped through the blockade.

Soon it sailed out into the open sea. The King's ships did not follow but went sadly back to Colchis.

The End of the Voyage

Many days later, the Argo came to an island. "We must stop here," Medea said. "This is the island where the enchantress Circe lives."

"She is my aunt and she has great magic powers. She will ask the gods to forgive me for killing Asbyrtus," she explained to Jason.

Jason and Medea went ashore to find Circe. Soon they came to a palace. A beautiful woman came out on to the marble steps to meet them.

"I am Circe," she said. "Why have you come?" "I killed my brother and I want the gods to forgive me. Please help us," said Medea.

Circe led them into her palace. Then she waved her magic wand over Medea and Jason. Suddenly there was a flash of light above them.

"The gods have forgiven you," Circe said. They thanked her and went back to the Argo. "Hoist the sails," cried Jason. "Now we can go home."

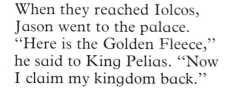

When they reached Iolcos, Jason went to the palace. "Here is the Golden Fleece," he said to King Pelias. "Now I claim my kingdom back."

"I thought the task was impossible," said the King. But he kept his promise and that night Jason and Medea were married and crowned

King and Queen of Iolcos. The whole city celebrated with feasting and dancing. And the Argonauts were glad their great voyage was over.

More about the story of Jason

The story of Jason and the Golden Fleece was first written down about 2,200 years ago by a poet called Apollonius of Rhodes. He wrote the story as a very long poem called "The Argonautica".

The city of Colchis was near the Caucasian Mountains in what is now Russia. It was about 2,000 kilometres by sea from Iolcos. The River Phasis flowed past it into the Black Sea, which was called the "Inhospitable Sea" by the Greeks as it had so few safe harbours. The ram landed at Colchis, so the story goes, because it was the most easterly place in the world.

The Greeks believed that the Golden Fleece was the coat of a flying ram. The ram rescued a little boy from his cruel step-mother and flew to Colchis with the boy on its back. The King of Colchis sacrificed the ram to the gods and hung its fleece on a tree.

The lyre which Orpheus played was given to him by Apollo, the god of music. Even the rocks and trees listened to his beautiful music and songs.

© Usborne Publishing Ltd
1991, 1982
First published in 1982 by
Usborne Publishing Ltd
Usborne House
83-85 Saffron Hill
London ECIN 8RT, England

Printed in Belgium.

The name of Usborne and the device are Trade Marks of Usborne Publishing Ltd.